Nathaniel Hawthorne (July 4, 1804 – May 19, 1864) was an American novelist, dark romantic, and short story writer. His works often focus on history, morality, and religion. He was born in 1804 in Salem, Massachusetts, to Nathaniel Hathorne and the former Elizabeth Clarke Manning. His ancestors include John Hathorne, the only judge involved in the Salem witch trials who never repented of his actions. He entered Bowdoin College in 1821, was elected to Phi Beta Kappa in 1824, and graduated in 1825. He published his first work in 1828, the novel Fanshawe; he later tried to suppress it, feeling that it was not equal to the standard of his later work. He published several short stories in periodicals, which he collected in 1837 as Twice-Told Tales. The next year, he became engaged to Sophia Peabody. He worked at the Boston Custom House and joined Brook Farm, a transcendentalist community, before marrying Peabody in 1842. The couple moved to The Old Manse in Concord, Massachusetts, later moving to Salem, the Berkshires, then to The Wayside in Concord. (Source: Wikipedia)

Literary works:

Fanshawe (published anonymously, 1828)
The New Adam and Eve (1843)
The Scarlet Letter (1850)
The House of the Seven Gables (1851)
The Blithedale Romance (1852)
The Marble Faun: Or, The Romance of Monte Beni (1860)
The Dolliver Romance (1863) (unfinished)
Septimius Felton; or, the Elixir of Life (unfinished)
Doctor Grimshawe's Secret: A Romance (unfinished, 1882)
Twice-Told Tales (1837)
Grandfather's Chair (1840)
Mosses from an Old Manse (1846)
A Wonder-Book for Girls and Boys (1851)
Tanglewood Tales (1853)

SKETCHES FROM MEMORY

NATHANIEL HAWTHORNE

PRINCE CLASSICS

PRINCE CLASSICS

This is a work of fiction. Names, characters, places, and incidents either are the product of the author's imagination or are used fictitiously. Any resemblance to actual persons, living or dead, events, or locales is entirely coincidental.

First Printing: 2020

ISBN 978-93-90027-66-8 (paperback)

ISBN 978-93-90027-67-5 (Hardcover)

Published by Prince Classics

www.princeclassics.com

Contents

SKETCHES FROM MEMORY

I. THE INLAND PORT.

It was a bright forenoon, when I set foot on the beach at Burlington, and took leave of the two boatmen in whose little skiff I had voyaged since daylight from Peru. Not that we had come that morning from South America, but only from the New York shore of Lake Champlain. The highlands of the coast behind us stretched north and south, in a double range of bold, blue peaks, gazing over each other's shoulders at the Green Mountains of Vermont.

The latter are far the loftiest, and, from the opposite side of the lake, had displayed a more striking outline. We were now almost at their feet, and could see only a sandy beach sweeping beneath a woody bank, around the semicircular Bay of Burlington.

The painted lighthouse on a small green island, the wharves and warehouses, with sloops and schooners moored alongside, or at anchor, or spreading their canvas to the wind, and boats rowing from point to point, reminded me of some fishing-town on the sea-coast.

But I had no need of tasting the water to convince myself that Lake Champlain was not all arm of the sea; its quality was evident, both by its silvery surface, when unruffled, and a faint but unpleasant and sickly smell, forever steaming up in the sunshine. One breeze of the Atlantic with its briny fragrance would be worth more to these inland people than all the perfumes of Arabia. On closer inspection the vessels at the wharves looked hardly seaworthy,—there being a great lack of tar about the seams and rigging, and perhaps other deficiencies, quite as much to the purpose.

I observed not a single sailor in the port. There were men, indeed, in blue jackets and trousers, but not of the true nautical fashion, such as dangle before slopshops; others wore tight pantaloons and coats preponderously long-tailed,—cutting very queer figures at the masthead; and, in short, these fresh-water fellows had about the same analogy to the real "old salt" with his tarpaulin, pea-jacket, and sailor-cloth trousers, as a lake fish to a Newfoundland cod.

Nothing struck me more in Burlington, than the great number of Irish emigrants. They have filled the British Provinces to the brim, and still continue to ascend the St. Lawrence in infinite tribes overflowing by every outlet into the States. At Burlington, they swarm in huts and mean dwellings near the lake, lounge about the wharves, and elbow the native citizens entirely out of competition in their own line. Every species of mere bodily labor is the prerogative of these Irish. Such is their multitude in comparison with any possible demand for their services, that it is difficult to conceive how a third part of them should earn even a daily glass of whiskey, which is doubtless their first necessary of life,—daily bread being only the second.

Some were angling in the lake, but had caught only a few perch, which little fishes, without a miracle, would be nothing among so many. A miracle there certainly must have been, and a daily one, for the subsistence of these wandering hordes. The men exhibit a lazy strength and careless merriment, as if they had fed well hitherto, and meant to feed better hereafter; the women strode about, uncovered in the open air, with far plumper waists and brawnier limbs as well as bolder faces, than our shy and slender females; and their progeny, which was innumerable, had the reddest and the roundest cheeks of any children in America.

While we stood at the wharf, the bell of a steamboat gave two preliminary peals, and she dashed away for Plattsburgh, leaving a trail of smoky breath behind, and breaking the glassy surface of the lake before her. Our next movement brought us into a handsome and busy square, the sides of which were filled up with white houses, brick stores, a church, a court-house, and a bank. Some of these edifices had roofs of tin, in the fashion of Montreal, and glittered in the sun with cheerful splendor, imparting a lively effect to the whole square. One brick building, designated in large letters as the custom-house, reminded us that this inland village is a port of entry, largely concerned in foreign trade and holding daily intercourse with the British empire. In this border country the Canadian bank-notes circulate as freely as our own, and British and American coin are jumbled into the same pocket, the effigies of the King of England being made to kiss those of the Goddess of Liberty.

Perhaps there was an emblem in the involuntary contact. There was a pleasant mixture of people in the square of Burlington, such as cannot be seen elsewhere, at one view; merchants from Montreal, British officers from the frontier garrisons, French Canadians, wandering Irish, Scotchmen of a better class, gentlemen of the South on a pleasure tour, country squires on business; and a great throng of Green Mountain boys, with their horse-wagons and ox-teams, true Yankees in aspect, and looking more superlatively so, by contrast with such a variety of foreigners.

II. ROCHESTER

The gray but transparent evening rather shaded than obscured the scene, leaving its stronger features visible, and even improved by the medium through which I beheld them. The volume of water is not very great, nor the roar deep enough to be termed grand, though such praise might have been appropriate before the good people of Rochester had abstracted a part of the unprofitable sublimity of the cascade. The Genesee has contributed so bountifully to their canals and mill-dams, that it approaches the precipice with diminished pomp, and rushes over it in foamy streams of various width, leaving a broad face of the rock insulated and unwashed, between the two main branches of the falling river. Still it was an impressive sight, to one who had not seen Niagara. I confess, however, that my chief interest arose from a legend, connected with these falls, which will become poetical in the lapse of years, and was already so to me as I pictured the catastrophe out of dusk and solitude. It was from a platform, raised over the naked island of the cliff, in the middle of the cataract that Sam Patch took his last leap, and alighted in the other world. Strange as it may appear,—that any uncertainty should rest upon his fate which was consummated in the sight of thousands,—many will tell you that the illustrious Patch concealed himself in a cave under the falls, and has continued to enjoy posthumous renown, without foregoing the comforts of this present life. But the poor fellow prized the shout of the multitude too much not to have claimed it at the instant, had he survived. He will not be seen again, unless his ghost, in such a twilight as when I was there, should emerge from the foam, and vanish among the shadows that fall from cliff to cliff.

How stern a moral may be drawn from the story of poor Sam Patch! Why do we call him a madman or a fool, when he has left his memory around the falls of the Genesee, more permanently than if the letters of his name had been hewn into the forehead of the precipice?

Was the leaper of cataracts more mad or foolish than other men who throw away life, or misspend it in pursuit of empty fame, and seldom so triumphantly as he? That which he won is as invaluable as any except the unsought glory, spreading like the rich perfume of richer fruit from various and useful deeds.

Thus musing, wise in theory, but practically as great a fool as Sam, I lifted my eyes and beheld the spires, warehouses, and dwellings of Rochester, half a mile distant on both sides of the river, indistinctly cheerful, with the twinkling of many lights amid the fall of the evening.

The town had sprung up like a mushroom, but no presage of decay could be drawn from its hasty growth. Its edifices are of dusky brick, and of stone that will not be grayer in a hundred years than now; its churches are Gothic; it is impossible to look at its worn pavements and conceive how lately the forest leaves have been swept away. The most ancient town in Massachusetts appears quite like an affair of yesterday, compared with Rochester. Its attributes of youth are the activity and eager life with which it is redundant. The whole street, sidewalks and centre, was crowded with pedestrians, horsemen, stage-coaches, gigs, light wagons, and heavy ox-teams, all hurrying, trotting, rattling, and rumbling, in a throng that passed continually, but never passed away. Here, a country wife was selecting a churn from several gayly painted ones on the sunny sidewalk; there, a farmer was bartering his produce; and, in two or three places, a crowd of people were showering bids on a vociferous auctioneer. I saw a great wagon and an ox-chain knocked off to a very pretty woman. Numerous were the lottery offices,—those true temples of Mammon,—where red and yellow bills offered splendid fortunes to the world at large, and banners of painted cloth gave notice that the "lottery draws next Wednesday." At the ringing of a bell, judges, jurymen, lawyers, and clients, elbowed each other to the court-house, to busy themselves with cases that would doubtless illustrate the state of society, had I the means of reporting them. The number of public houses benefited the flow of temporary population; some were farmer's taverns,—cheap, homely, and comfortable; others were magnificent hotels, with negro waiters, gentlemanly landlords in black broad-cloth, and foppish bar-keepers in Broadway coats, with chased gold watches in their waistcoat-pockets. I caught one of these fellows quizzing me through an eye-glass. The porters were lumbering up the steps with baggage from the packet boats, while waiters plied the brush on dusty travellers, who, meanwhile, glanced over the innumerable advertisements in the daily papers.

In short, everybody seemed to be there, and all had something to do, and were doing it with all their might, except a party of drunken recruits for the Western military posts, principally Irish and Scotch, though they wore Uncle Sam's gray jacket and trousers. I noticed one other idle man. He carried a rifle on his shoulder and a powder-horn across his breast, and appeared to stare about him with confused wonder, as if, while he was listening to the wind among the forest boughs, the hum and bustle of an instantaneous city had surrounded him.

III. A NIGHT SCENE

The steamboat in which I was passenger for Detroit had put into the mouth of a small river, where the greater part of the night would be spent in repairing some damages of the machinery.

As the evening was warm, though cloudy and very dark, I stood on deck, watching a scene that would not have attracted a second glance in the daytime, but became picturesque by the magic of strong light and deep shade.

Some wild Irishmen were replenishing our stock of wood, and had kindled a great fire on the bank to illuminate their labors. It was composed of large logs and dry brushwood, heaped together with careless profusion, blazing fiercely, spouting showers of sparks into the darkness, and gleaming wide over Lake Erie,—a beacon for perplexed voyagers leagues from land.

All around and above the furnace, there was total obscurity. No trees or other objects caught and reflected any portion of the brightness, which thus wasted itself in the immense void of night, as if it quivered from the expiring embers of the world, after the final conflagration. But the Irishmen were continually emerging from the dense gloom, passing through the lurid glow, and vanishing into the gloom on the other side. Sometimes a whole figure would be made visible, by the shirtsleeves and light-colored dress; others were but half seen, like imperfect creatures; many flitted, shadow-like, along the skirts of darkness, tempting fancy to a vain pursuit; and often, a face alone was reddened by the fire, and stared strangely distinct, with no traces of a body. In short these wild Irish, distorted and exaggerated by the blaze, now lost in deep shadow, now bursting into sudden splendor, and now struggling between light and darkness, formed a picture which might have been transferred, almost unaltered, to a tale of the supernatural. As they all carried lanterns of wood, and often flung sticks upon the fire, the least imaginative spectator would at once compare them to devils condemned to keep alive the flames of their own torments.

About Author

Nathaniel Hawthorne (**Hathorne**; July 4, 1804 – May 19, 1864) was an American novelist, dark romantic, and short story writer. His works often focus on history, morality, and religion.

He was born in 1804 in Salem, Massachusetts, to Nathaniel Hathorne and the former Elizabeth Clarke Manning. His ancestors include John Hathorne, the only judge involved in the Salem witch trials who never repented of his actions. He entered Bowdoin College in 1821, was elected to Phi Beta Kappa in 1824, and graduated in 1825. He published his first work in 1828, the novel Fanshawe; he later tried to suppress it, feeling that it was not equal to the standard of his later work. He published several short stories in periodicals, which he collected in 1837 as Twice-Told Tales. The next year, he became engaged to Sophia Peabody. He worked at the Boston Custom House and joined Brook Farm, a transcendentalist community, before marrying Peabody in 1842. The couple moved to The Old Manse in Concord, Massachusetts, later moving to Salem, the Berkshires, then to The Wayside in Concord. The Scarlet Letter was published in 1850, followed by a succession of other novels. A political appointment as consul took Hawthorne and family to Europe before their return to Concord in 1860. Hawthorne died on May 19, 1864, and was survived by his wife and their three children.

Much of Hawthorne's writing centers on New England, many works featuring moral metaphors with an anti-Puritan inspiration. His fiction works are considered part of the Romantic movement and, more specifically, dark romanticism. His themes often center on the inherent evil and sin of humanity, and his works often have moral messages and deep psychological complexity. His published works include novels, short stories, and a biography of his college friend Franklin Pierce, the 14th President of the United States.

Biography

Early life

Nathaniel Hawthorne was born on July 4, 1804, in Salem, Massachusetts;

his birthplace is preserved and open to the public. William Hathorne was the author's great-great-great-grandfather. He was a Puritan and was the first of the family to emigrate from England, settling in Dorchester, Massachusetts, before moving to Salem. There he became an important member of the Massachusetts Bay Colony and held many political positions, including magistrate and judge, becoming infamous for his harsh sentencing. William's son and the author's great-great-grandfather John Hathorne was one of the judges who oversaw the Salem witch trials. Hawthorne probably added the "w" to his surname in his early twenties, shortly after graduating from college, in an effort to dissociate himself from his notorious forebears. Hawthorne's father Nathaniel Hathorne Sr. was a sea captain who died in 1808 of yellow fever in Suriname; he had been a member of the East India Marine Society. After his death, his widow moved with young Nathaniel and two daughters to live with relatives named the Mannings in Salem, where they lived for 10 years. Young Hawthorne was hit on the leg while playing "bat and ball" on November 10, 1813, and he became lame and bedridden for a year, though several physicians could find nothing wrong with him.

In the summer of 1816, the family lived as boarders with farmers before moving to a home recently built specifically for them by Hawthorne's uncles Richard and Robert Manning in Raymond, Maine, near Sebago Lake. Years later, Hawthorne looked back at his time in Maine fondly: "Those were delightful days, for that part of the country was wild then, with only scattered clearings, and nine tenths of it primeval woods." In 1819, he was sent back to Salem for school and soon complained of homesickness and being too far from his mother and sisters. He distributed seven issues of The Spectator to his family in August and September 1820 for the sake of having fun. The homemade newspaper was written by hand and included essays, poems, and news featuring the young author's adolescent humor.

Hawthorne's uncle Robert Manning insisted that the boy attend college, despite Hawthorne's protests. With the financial support of his uncle, Hawthorne was sent to Bowdoin College in 1821, partly because of family connections in the area, and also because of its relatively inexpensive tuition rate. Hawthorne met future president Franklin Pierce on the way to

Bowdoin, at the stage stop in Portland, and the two became fast friends. Once at the school, he also met future poet Henry Wadsworth Longfellow, future congressman Jonathan Cilley, and future naval reformer Horatio Bridge. He graduated with the class of 1825, and later described his college experience to Richard Henry Stoddard:

> I was educated (as the phrase is) at Bowdoin College. I was an idle student, negligent of college rules and the Procrustean details of academic life, rather choosing to nurse my own fancies than to dig into Greek roots and be numbered among the learned Thebans.

Early career

In 1836, Hawthorne served as the editor of the American Magazine of Useful and Entertaining Knowledge. At the time, he boarded with poet Thomas Green Fessenden on Hancock Street in Beacon Hill in Boston. He was offered an appointment as weigher and gauger at the Boston Custom House at a salary of $1,500 a year, which he accepted on January 17, 1839. During his time there, he rented a room from George Stillman Hillard, business partner of Charles Sumner. Hawthorne wrote in the comparative obscurity of what he called his "owl's nest" in the family home. As he looked back on this period of his life, he wrote: "I have not lived, but only dreamed about living." He contributed short stories to various magazines and annuals, including "Young Goodman Brown" and "The Minister's Black Veil", though none drew major attention to him. Horatio Bridge offered to cover the risk of collecting these stories in the spring of 1837 into the volume Twice-Told Tales, which made Hawthorne known locally.

Marriage and family

While at Bowdoin, Hawthorne wagered a bottle of Madeira wine with his friend Jonathan Cilley that Cilley would get married before Hawthorne did. By 1836, he had won the bet, but he did not remain a bachelor for life. He had public flirtations with Mary Silsbee and Elizabeth Peabody, then he began pursuing Peabody's sister, illustrator and transcendentalist Sophia Peabody. He joined the transcendentalist Utopian community at Brook Farm in 1841, not because he agreed with the experiment but because it helped him save money to marry Sophia. He paid a $1,000 deposit and was put in charge of shoveling the hill of manure referred to as "the Gold Mine". He left later that year, though his Brook Farm adventure became an inspiration for his novel The Blithedale Romance. Hawthorne married Sophia Peabody on July 9, 1842, at a ceremony in the Peabody parlor on West Street in Boston. The couple moved to The Old Manse in Concord, Massachusetts, where they lived for three years. His neighbor Ralph Waldo Emerson invited him into his social circle, but Hawthorne was almost pathologically shy and stayed silent at gatherings. At the Old Manse, Hawthorne wrote most of the tales collected in Mosses from an Old Manse.

Like Hawthorne, Sophia was a reclusive person. Throughout her early life, she had frequent migraines and underwent several experimental medical treatments. She was mostly bedridden until her sister introduced her to Hawthorne, after which her headaches seem to have abated. The Hawthornes enjoyed a long and happy marriage. He referred to her as his "Dove" and wrote that she "is, in the strictest sense, my sole companion; and I need no other—there is no vacancy in my mind, any more than in my heart ... Thank God that I suffice for her boundless heart!" Sophia greatly admired her husband's work. She wrote in one of her journals:

> I am always so dazzled and bewildered with the richness, the depth, the ... jewels of beauty in his productions that I am always looking forward to a second reading where I can ponder and muse and fully take in the miraculous wealth of thoughts.

Poet Ellery Channing came to the Old Manse for help on the first anniversary of the Hawthornes' marriage. A local teenager named Martha Hunt had drowned herself in the river and Hawthorne's boat Pond Lily was needed to find her body. Hawthorne helped recover the corpse, which he described as "a spectacle of such perfect horror ... She was the very image of death-agony". The incident later inspired a scene in his novel The Blithedale Romance.

The Hawthornes had three children. Their first was daughter Una, born March 3, 1844; her name was a reference to The Faerie Queene, to the displeasure of family members. Hawthorne wrote to a friend, "I find it a very sober and serious kind of happiness that springs from the birth of a child ... There is no escaping it any longer. I have business on earth now, and must look about me for the means of doing it." In October 1845, the Hawthornes moved to Salem. In 1846, their son Julian was born. Hawthorne wrote to his sister Louisa on June 22, 1846: "A small troglodyte made his appearance here at ten minutes to six o'clock this morning, who claimed to be your nephew." Daughter Rose was born in May 1851, and Hawthorne called her his "autumnal flower".

Middle years

In April 1846, Hawthorne was officially appointed the Surveyor for the District of Salem and Beverly and Inspector of the Revenue for the Port of Salem at an annual salary of $1,200. He had difficulty writing during this period, as he admitted to Longfellow:

> I am trying to resume my pen ... Whenever I sit alone, or walk alone, I find myself dreaming about stories, as of old; but these forenoons in the Custom House undo all that the afternoons and evenings have done. I should be happier if I could write.

This employment, like his earlier appointment to the custom house in Boston, was vulnerable to the politics of the spoils system. Hawthorne was a Democrat and lost this job due to the change of administration in Washington after the presidential election of 1848. He wrote a letter of protest to the Boston Daily Advertiser which was attacked by the Whigs and supported by the Democrats, making Hawthorne's dismissal a much-talked about event in New England. He was deeply affected by the death of his mother in late July, calling it "the darkest hour I ever lived". He was appointed the corresponding secretary of the Salem Lyceum in 1848. Guests who came to speak that season included Emerson, Thoreau, Louis Agassiz, and Theodore Parker.

Hawthorne returned to writing and published The Scarlet Letter in mid-March 1850, including a preface that refers to his three-year tenure in the Custom House and makes several allusions to local politicians—who did not appreciate their treatment. It was one of the first mass-produced books in America, selling 2,500 volumes within ten days and earning Hawthorne $1,500 over 14 years. The book was pirated by booksellers in London and became a best-seller in the United States; it initiated his most lucrative period as a writer. Hawthorne's friend Edwin Percy Whipple objected to the novel's "morbid intensity" and its dense psychological details, writing that the book "is therefore apt to become, like Hawthorne, too painfully anatomical in his exhibition of them", though 20th-century writer D. H. Lawrence said that there could be no more perfect work of the American imagination than The Scarlet Letter.

Hawthorne and his family moved to a small red farmhouse near Lenox, Massachusetts, at the end of March 1850. He became friends with Herman Melville beginning on August 5, 1850, when the authors met at a picnic hosted by a mutual friend. Melville had just read Hawthorne's short story collection Mosses from an Old Manse, and his unsigned review of the collection was printed in The Literary World on August 17 and August 24 titled "Hawthorne and His Mosses". Melville wrote that these stories revealed a dark side to Hawthorne, "shrouded in blackness, ten times black". He was composing his novel Moby-Dick at the time, and dedicated the work in 1851 to Hawthorne: "In token of my admiration for his genius, this book is inscribed to Nathaniel Hawthorne."

Hawthorne's time in the Berkshires was very productive. While there, he wrote The House of the Seven Gables (1851), which poet and critic James Russell Lowell said was better than The Scarlet Letter and called "the most valuable contribution to New England history that has been made." He also wrote The Blithedale Romance (1852), his only work written in the first person. He also published A Wonder-Book for Girls and Boys in 1851, a collection of short stories retelling myths which he had been thinking about writing since 1846. Nevertheless, poet Ellery Channing reported that Hawthorne "has suffered much living in this place". The family enjoyed the scenery of the Berkshires, although Hawthorne did not enjoy the winters in their small house. They left on November 21, 1851. Hawthorne noted, "I am sick to death of Berkshire ... I have felt languid and dispirited, during almost my whole residence."

The Wayside and Europe

In May 1852, the Hawthornes returned to Concord where they lived until July 1853. In February, they bought The Hillside, a home previously inhabited by Amos Bronson Alcott and his family, and renamed it The Wayside. Their neighbors in Concord included Emerson and Henry David Thoreau.That year, Hawthorne wrote The Life of Franklin Pierce, the campaign biography of his friend which depicted him as "a man of peaceful pursuits". Horace Mann said, "If he makes out Pierce to be a great man or a brave man, it will be the greatest work of fiction he ever wrote." In the biography, Hawthorne depicts Pierce as a statesman and soldier who had accomplished no great feats because of his need to make "little noise" and so "withdrew into the background". He also left out Pierce's drinking habits, despite rumors of his alcoholism, and emphasized Pierce's belief that slavery could not "be remedied by human contrivances" but would, over time, "vanish like a dream".

With Pierce's election as President, Hawthorne was rewarded in 1853 with the position of United States consul in Liverpool shortly after the publication of Tanglewood Tales.The role was considered the most lucrative foreign service position at the time, described by Hawthorne's wife as "second in dignity to the Embassy in London". His appointment ended in 1857 at the close of the Pierce administration, and the Hawthorne family toured France and Italy. During his time in Italy, the previously clean-shaven Hawthorne grew a bushy mustache.

The family returned to The Wayside in 1860, and that year saw the publication of The Marble Faun, his first new book in seven years. Hawthorne admitted that he had aged considerably, referring to himself as "wrinkled with time and trouble".

Later years and death

At the outset of the American Civil War, Hawthorne traveled with William D. Ticknor to Washington, D.C., where he met Abraham Lincoln and other notable figures. He wrote about his experiences in the essay "Chiefly About War Matters" in 1862.

Failing health prevented him from completing several more romance novels. Hawthorne was suffering from pain in his stomach and insisted on a recuperative trip with his friend Franklin Pierce, though his neighbor Bronson Alcott was concerned that Hawthorne was too ill. While on a tour of the White Mountains, he died in his sleep on May 19, 1864, in Plymouth, New Hampshire. Pierce sent a telegram to Elizabeth Peabody asking her to inform Mrs. Hawthorne in person. Mrs. Hawthorne was too saddened by the news to handle the funeral arrangements herself. Hawthorne's son Julian was a freshman at Harvard College, and he learned of his father's death the next day; coincidentally, he was initiated into the Delta Kappa Epsilon fraternity on the same day by being blindfolded and placed in a coffin.Longfellow wrote a tribute poem to Hawthorne published in 1866 called "The Bells of Lynn". Hawthorne was buried on what is now known as "Authors' Ridge" in Sleepy Hollow Cemetery, Concord, Massachusetts. Pallbearers included Longfellow, Emerson, Alcott, Oliver Wendell Holmes Sr., James Thomas Fields, and Edwin Percy Whipple. Emerson wrote of the funeral: "I thought there was a tragic element in the event, that might be more fully rendered—in the painful solitude of the man, which, I suppose, could no longer be endured, & he died of it."

His wife Sophia and daughter Una were originally buried in England. However, in June 2006, they were reinterred in plots adjacent to Hawthorne.

Writings

Hawthorne had a particularly close relationship with his publishers William Ticknor and James Thomas Fields. Hawthorne once told Fields, "I care more for your good opinion than for that of a host of critics." In fact, it was Fields who convinced Hawthorne to turn The Scarlet Letter into a novel rather than a short story. Ticknor handled many of Hawthorne's personal matters, including the purchase of cigars, overseeing financial accounts, and even purchasing clothes. Ticknor died with Hawthorne at his side in Philadelphia in 1864; according to a friend, Hawthorne was left "apparently dazed".

Literary style and themes

Hawthorne's works belong to romanticism or, more specifically, dark romanticism, cautionary tales that suggest that guilt, sin, and evil are the most inherent natural qualities of humanity. Many of his works are inspired by Puritan New England, combining historical romance loaded with symbolism and deep psychological themes, bordering on surrealism. His depictions of the past are a version of historical fiction used only as a vehicle to express common themes of ancestral sin, guilt and retribution. His later writings also reflect his negative view of the Transcendentalism movement.

Hawthorne was predominantly a short story writer in his early career. Upon publishing Twice-Told Tales, however, he noted, "I do not think much of them," and he expected little response from the public. His four major romances were written between 1850 and 1860: The Scarlet Letter (1850), The House of the Seven Gables (1851), The Blithedale Romance (1852) and The Marble Faun (1860). Another novel-length romance, Fanshawe, was published anonymously in 1828. Hawthorne defined a romance as being radically different from a novel by not being concerned with the possible or probable course of ordinary experience. In the preface to The House of the Seven Gables, Hawthorne describes his romance-writing as using "atmospherical medium as to bring out or mellow the lights and deepen and enrich the shadows of the picture". The picture, Daniel Hoffman found, was one of "the primitive energies of fecundity and creation."

Critics have applied feminist perspectives and historicist approaches to Hawthorne's depictions of women. Feminist scholars are interested particularly in Hester Prynne: they recognize that while she herself could not be the "destined prophetess" of the future, the "angel and apostle of the coming revelation" must nevertheless "be a woman." Camille Paglia saw Hester as mystical, "a wandering goddess still bearing the mark of her Asiatic origins ... moving serenely in the magic circle of her sexual nature". Lauren Berlant termed Hester "the citizen as woman [personifying] love as a quality of the body that contains the purest light of nature," her resulting "traitorous political theory" a "Female Symbolic" literalization of futile Puritan metaphors. Historicists view Hester as a protofeminist and avatar of the self-reliance and responsibility that led to women's suffrage and reproductive emancipation. Anthony Splendora found her literary genealogy among other archetypally fallen but redeemed women, both historic and mythic. As examples, he offers Psyche of ancient legend; Heloise of twelfth-century France's tragedy involving world-renowned philosopher Peter Abelard; Anne Hutchinson (America's first heretic, circa 1636), and Hawthorne family friend Margaret Fuller. In Hester's first appearance, Hawthorne likens her, "infant at her bosom", to Mary, Mother of Jesus, "the image of Divine Maternity". In her study of Victorian literature, in which such "galvanic outcasts" as Hester feature prominently, Nina Auerbach went so far as to name Hester's fall and subsequent redemption, "the novel's one unequivocally religious activity". Regarding Hester as a deity figure, Meredith A. Powers found in Hester's characterization "the earliest in American fiction that the archetypal Goddess appears quite graphically," like a Goddess "not the wife of traditional marriage, permanently subject to a male overlord"; Powers noted "her syncretism, her flexibility, her inherent ability to alter and so avoid the defeat of secondary status in a goal-oriented civilization".

Aside from Hester Prynne, the model women of Hawthorne's other novels—from Ellen Langton of Fanshawe to Zenobia and Priscilla of The Blithedale Romance, Hilda and Miriam of The Marble Faun and Phoebe and Hepzibah of The House of the Seven Gables—are more fully realized than his male characters, who merely orbit them. This observation is equally true of his short-stories, in which central females serve as allegorical figures: Rappaccini's beautiful but life-altering, garden-bound, daughter; almost-perfect Georgiana of "The Birthmark"; the sinned-against (abandoned) Ester of "Ethan Brand"; and goodwife Faith Brown, linchpin of Young Goodman Brown's very belief in God. "My Faith is gone!" Brown exclaims in despair upon seeing his wife at the Witches' Sabbath. Perhaps the most sweeping statement of Hawthorne's impetus comes from Mark Van Doren: "Somewhere, if not in the New England of his time, Hawthorne unearthed the image of a goddess supreme in beauty and power."

Hawthorne also wrote nonfiction. In 2008, the Library of America selected Hawthorne's "A show of wax-figures" for inclusion in its two-century retrospective of American True Crime.

Criticism

In "Hawthorne and His Mosses", Herman Melville wrote a passionate argument for Hawthorne to be among the burgeoning American literary canon, "He is one of the new, and far better generation of your writers." In this review of Mosses from an Old Manse, Melville describes an affinity for Hawthorne that would only increase: "I feel that this Hawthorne has dropped germinous seeds into my soul. He expands and deepens down, the more I contemplate him; and further, and further, shoots his strong New-England roots into the hot soil of my Southern soul." Edgar Allan Poe wrote important reviews of both Twice-Told Tales and Mosses from an Old Manse. Poe's assessment was partly informed by his contempt of allegory and moral tales, and his chronic accusations of plagiarism, though he admitted,

> The style of Mr. Hawthorne is purity itself. His tone is singularly effective—wild, plaintive, thoughtful, and in full accordance with his themes ... We look upon him as one of the few men of indisputable genius to whom our country has as yet given birth.

Ralph Waldo Emerson wrote, "Nathaniel Hawthorne's reputation as a writer is a very pleasing fact, because his writing is not good for anything, and this is a tribute to the man." Henry James praised Hawthorne, saying, "The fine thing in Hawthorne is that he cared for the deeper psychology, and that, in his way, he tried to become familiar with it." Poet John Greenleaf Whittier wrote that he admired the "weird and subtle beauty" in Hawthorne's tales. Evert Augustus Duyckinck said of Hawthorne, "Of the American writers destined to live, he is the most original, the one least indebted to foreign models or literary precedents of any kind."

Contemporary response to Hawthorne's work praised his sentimentality and moral purity while more modern evaluations focus on the dark psychological complexity. Beginning in the 1950s, critics have focused on symbolism and didacticism.

The critic Harold Bloom opined that only Henry James and William Faulkner challenge Hawthorne's position as the greatest American novelist, although he admitted that he favored James as the greatest American novelist.

Bloom saw Hawthorne's greatest works to be principally The Scarlet Letter, followed by The Marble Faun and certain short stories, including "My Kinsman, Major Molineux", "Young Goodman Brown", "Wakefield", and "Feathertop". (Source: Wikipedia)

NOTABLE WORKS

NOVELS

Fanshawe (published anonymously, 1828)

The Scarlet Letter (1850)

The House of the Seven Gables (1851)

The Blithedale Romance (1852)

The Marble Faun: Or, The Romance of Monte Beni (1860) (as Transformation: Or, The Romance of Monte Beni, UK publication, same year)

The Dolliver Romance (1863) (unfinished)

Septimius Felton; or, the Elixir of Life (unfinished, published in the Atlantic Monthly, 1872)

Doctor Grimshawe's Secret: A Romance (unfinished, with preface and notes by Julian Hawthorne, 1882)

SHORT STORY COLLECTIONS

Twice-Told Tales (1837)

Grandfather's Chair (1840)

Mosses from an Old Manse (1846)

A Wonder-Book for Girls and Boys (1851)

The Snow-Image, and Other Twice-Told Tales (1852)

Tanglewood Tales (1853)

The Dolliver Romance and Other Pieces (1876)

The Great Stone Face and Other Tales of the White Mountains (1889)

SELECTED SHORT STORIES

"The Hollow of the Three Hills" (1830)

"Roger Malvin's Burial" (1832)

"My Kinsman, Major Molineux" (1832)

"The Minister's Black Veil" (1832)

"Young Goodman Brown" (1835)

"The Gray Champion" (1835)

"The White Old Maid" (1835)

"Wakefield" (1835)

"The Ambitious Guest" (1835)

"The Man of Adamant" (1837)

"The May-Pole of Merry Mount" (1837)

"The Great Carbuncle" (1837)

"Dr. Heidegger's Experiment" (1837)

"A Virtuoso's Collection" (May 1842)

"The Birth-Mark" (March 1843)

"The Celestial Railroad" (1843)

"Egotism; or, The Bosom-Serpent" (1843)

"Earth's Holocaust" (1844)

"Rappaccini's Daughter" (1844)

"P.'s Correspondence" (1845)

"The Artist of the Beautiful" (1846)

"Fire Worship" (1846)

"Ethan Brand" (1850)

"The Great Stone Face" (1850)

"Feathertop" (1852)

NONFICTION

Twenty Days with Julian & Little Bunny (written 1851, published 1904)

Our Old Home (1863)

Passages from the French and Italian Notebooks (1871)

CPSIA information can be obtained
at www.ICGtesting.com
Printed in the USA
LVHW090148160720
660560LV00012BA/417

9 789390 027675